The Pet Keeper Fairies

For the fabulous Molly Shanahan,
with love

Special thanks to
Narinder Dhami

ORCHARD BOOKS
338 Euston Road, London NW1 3BH
Orchard Books
Hachette Children's Books
Level 17/207 Kent Street, Sydney, NSW 2000
A Paperback Original

First published in Great Britain in 2006
Rainbow Magic is a registered trademark of Working Partners Limited.
Series created by Working Partners Limited, London W6 OQT

ISBN 1 84616 172 X
1 3 5 7 9 10 8 6 4 2

Printed and bound in China

Molly
the Goldfish
Fairy

by Daisy Meadows

illustrated by Georgie Ripper

ORCHARD BOOKS

www.rainbowmagic.co.uk

Fairies with their pets I see
And yet no pet has chosen me!
So I will get some of my own
To share my perfect frosty home.

This spell I cast. Its aim is clear:
To bring the magic pets straight here.
Pet Keeper Fairies soon will see
Their seven pets living with me!

Contents

Gnome, Sweet Gnome   9

Gnomes Alive   23

Flash Has Some Fun   35

Kirsty's Challenge   47

Tug-of-War   55

Winner Takes All   67

Gnome, Sweet Gnome

"Slow down, Dad," Kirsty Tate
called. "You're leaving us behind!"

"Sorry," Mr Tate stopped and
waited for Kirsty, Rachel and
Mrs Tate to catch up. "I'm feeling
hungry, and you know how good
the Wainwrights' barbecues
always are. In fact..." He sniffed the

air. "I think I can smell the food cooking from here!"

"We're still two streets away!" Kirsty said, grinning and shaking her head at her best friend Rachel who burst out laughing.

Mr and Mrs Tate walked on and the girls followed.

"We'll have a good time at the barbecue," Kirsty said, smiling at Rachel who was staying with her for the holidays. "The Wainwrights have got a huge garden. It's lovely."

"Great!" Rachel said eagerly. Then she lowered her voice. "Don't forget, we must look out for fairy pets!"

Kirsty nodded. "The fairies are depending on us," she whispered.

Rachel and Kirsty had never told anyone their very special secret. They had become friends with the fairies and now, whenever their magical friends were in trouble, the girls always tried to help. Jack Frost often caused problems in Fairyland, and now he had stolen the seven magic animals belonging to the Pet Keeper Fairies. But the

mischievous pets had managed to
escape from Jack Frost and his goblin
servants into the human world. Rachel
and Kirsty were determined to find all
the pets and restore them to their fairy
owners before the goblins captured
them and took them back to Jack
Frost again.

"Well, we've found five pets," Kirsty
went on, as they turned into
the Wainwrights' street.
"Yes, we've just
got the goldfish
and the pony left to
find," Rachel agreed
thoughtfully. "The
goldfish will be tricky.
It's the smallest pet
we've had to look for!"

"Here we are," Mrs Tate announced, opening a little white gate. "The Wainwrights said to go straight round to the back garden."

Rachel and Kirsty could smell the food cooking as they walked round the side of the house, and it made their mouths water.

"Caroline," Mrs Tate called, as they entered the back garden. "Paul, we're here!"

A barbecue stood on the patio next to the house. Smoke curled from it as sausages sizzled.

13

A tall man wearing a blue apron turned to beam at them all.

"Hello, everyone," Mr Wainwright said, waving a fork.

"Oh!" Rachel gasped with delight as she walked onto the patio. "What a gorgeous garden!"

The garden was very long and wide,
with an emerald-green lawn dotted
with flowerbeds of bushes and colourful,
scented flowers. Brick paths wove in
and out of the flowerbeds, one of
them leading to a large fish pond,
half-hidden by weeping willow trees
at the end of the garden.

Mr Wainwright grinned. "You must be Kirsty's friend, Rachel," he said.

Rachel nodded. "Your garden's beautiful," she told him eagerly.

Mr Wainwright looked pleased. "Thank you," he said. "Has Kirsty told you about my prize collection?"

"What's that?" Rachel asked, puzzled.

Kirsty laughed. "Mr Wainwright collects garden gnomes," she explained. "There are lots of them hidden around the garden. When I was little, I used to spend ages looking for them."

"Come and see my latest." Mr Wainwright led them over to the picnic

table and pointed at the nearby
rockery. "Isn't he a beauty?"

A rosy-cheeked gnome sat at a little
table among the rocks. He looked deep
in thought, stroking his white beard as
he stared at a draughts board in front
of him.

"He's lovely!" said Rachel.

"And he looks just like Paul does
when he's thinking!" laughed a voice
behind them.

The girls turned to see that Mrs Wainwright had just come out of the kitchen.

"Hello, everyone," she said, smiling. "It's nice to meet you, Rachel. I'm sure Kirsty will show you round the garden, so that you can see our other gnomes."

"Oh, yes!" Kirsty said eagerly. "I'll show Rachel the fish pond too."

"We've just bought a new goldfish called Rusty," Mr Wainwright chimed in. "So we have five fish now."

Mr and Mrs Tate began
to help the Wainwrights
with the food, while
Kirsty led Rachel
down the garden.

"Can you spot the
gnomes?" Kirsty
asked, pointing.

"There's one
with a kite by the
summerhouse," Rachel
laughed. "One on
a motorbike by the shed. Ooh,
and there's one in that flowerbed holding
a tennis racket. They're everywhere!"

Kirsty nodded, grinning. "There are
more by the pond," she said, heading
in that direction. "Let's go and look
at the fish."

Rachel followed, and peered into the water.

"The black fish is called Shadow," Kirsty explained, "and the white one with red spots is Clown." She leaned over the water and pointed. "Can you see the red fish with white spots? That's Flame. And the little speckled one is Spots."

Rachel nodded. "That's four," she counted. Then she noticed a bright orange fish. "That must be the new fish, Rusty," she added.

Kirsty nodded, but Rachel blinked. For a moment she thought she'd seen a sixth fish! Rachel bent over the pool and looked more closely. There it was again: a beautiful golden fish that seemed to shimmer as it swam through the water – almost as if it was sparkling with fairy magic!

Gnomes Alive!

"Kirsty!" Rachel gasped, hardly able to believe her eyes. "Did you see that?"

"What?" asked Kirsty. She'd been watching Flame and Spots and hadn't noticed a thing.

"A sixth fish!" Rachel said.

Kirsty looked puzzled. "But Mr Wainwright said there were only five fish," she murmured, frowning. But then, suddenly, she spotted the golden fish herself; its shining tail moving gracefully in the water.

"Look!" Rachel exclaimed, seeing it too. "See how it's shimmering?"

Kirsty's eyes opened wide. The fish seemed to be casting a golden light which sparkled across the surface of the pond.

"Fairy magic!" Kirsty breathed excitedly. "Rachel, do you think this could be Molly the Goldfish Fairy's pet?"

Rachel nodded, looking thrilled. "I'm sure it is!" she declared.

"What shall we do?" asked Kirsty, keeping a close watch on the magical fish. "Should we catch him?"

"Maybe Molly's not too far away," Rachel said, turning to look around the garden.

Just then Kirsty noticed something move out of the corner of her eye. Sitting on a rock at the side of the pond was a garden gnome dipping a fishing-net into the water. As Kirsty looked, she thought she saw the gnome's arm move. Then, to Kirsty's amazement, the gnome suddenly jumped to his feet! Kirsty blinked several times, wondering if she was seeing things. "Rachel," she whispered urgently. "The gnome by the pond has just come alive!"

Puzzled, Rachel turned to look. Sure enough, a gnome was bending over the pond, chuckling to himself. But then Rachel's heart missed a beat. This was no ordinary garden gnome. This gnome was green all over, with a pointy nose and very big feet!

"That's not a gnome," Rachel hissed. "It's a goblin!"

Kirsty stared at the gnome and realised that her friend was right. "Oh, no!" she gasped.

So far, the goblin hadn't noticed the girls because they were half-hidden by a large bush. Rachel pulled Kirsty further out of sight, and then the girls peeped out between the leaves.

Suddenly, the goblin gave a great roar of triumph. "I've caught the magic goldfish!" he called, lifting his fishing-net out of the water.

Rachel and Kirsty stared in dismay as the goblin tipped the contents of the net into a jam jar at his side. The jar glowed with golden light as the fairy pet fell into the water and began swimming round in circles.

"Ha ha!" the goblin giggled smugly,

picking up the jam jar and dancing around with it. "I'm the cleverest goblin of all! Jack Frost will be pleased with me!"

Rachel and Kirsty jumped as another goblin popped out of a bush close by.

"Let me see the magic goldfish!" he cried. He too was disguised as a garden gnome, dressed as a golfer and carrying a little bag of golf clubs.

"Me too!" called another goblin.

"Let me hold the jam jar!"
demanded yet another.

Kirsty and Rachel could hardly
believe their eyes as goblins, disguised
as gnomes, came dashing towards the
pond from every direction. One had
a wheelbarrow, one held a spade and
two were wearing kilts and carrying

bagpipes! They all dropped whatever they were holding and crowded round the jam jar.

"They've been hiding in the Wainwrights' garden disguised as gnomes!" Rachel whispered.

Kirsty nodded. "We must get Molly's goldfish back quickly," she said urgently.

"Come on, Rachel!"

Looking determined, Rachel and Kirsty stepped out from behind the shrub.

The golfer goblin spotted them first. "It's those pesky girls again!" he shouted.

"Put that goldfish back in the pond!" Kirsty said firmly, marching towards the goblins with Rachel right behind her. "No way!" the goblin said, putting the jam jar behind his back and glaring at the girls. "We're taking it to Jack Frost."

"So there!" added the goblin with the wheelbarrow. He blew a huge raspberry at the girls, and the other goblins roared with laughter. Then, before Rachel and Kirsty could say or do anything else, all the goblins turned and ran away.

Flash Has Some Fun

"After them, Kirsty!" Rachel exclaimed.

But just then, the girls heard a tiny, silvery voice above them cry, "Wheeeee!"

Rachel and Kirsty looked up. Molly the Goldfish Fairy was swooping through the air towards them. She wore a turquoise skirt and a blue top,

and her long red curls were held back
by a band of blue roses. A sparkling
glass fishbowl full of water swung from
her arm like a tiny shining handbag.

"Molly!" Kirsty said in delight.

Molly hovered in front of the girls.
"I'm so glad to see you," she declared,
beaming at Rachel and Kirsty. "I have
a feeling my darling Flash is around
here somewhere. Have you seen him?"

"The goblins have got him!" Rachel said, pointing to the very end of the garden, where the goblins were standing by the fence, arguing about how they were going to climb over it with the jam jar.

"They fished him out of the pond and now he's trapped in the jar," explained Kirsty.

Molly laughed. "That's not a problem for Flash," she said. "Watch." She fluttered up into the air again. "Flash!" she called. "Here, boy!"

Rachel and Kirsty saw a sparkling shimmer swirl up inside the jam jar.

The next moment, Flash leapt out and began to swim towards them – through the air!

"That's amazing!" Rachel gasped.

"I know," Molly laughed. "Isn't he cool? Of course, real fish have to stay in water, but because Flash is magic he can swim in the air as well!"

"Hey!" The goblin holding the jam jar had suddenly noticed it was empty. "Where's the fish gone?"

"He's getting away!" another goblin shouted, spotting Flash swimming through the air. "After him!"

The goblins chased after Flash, tumbling over their own feet as they ran.

The golfer goblin was faster than the others. He caught up with Flash and made a grab for the little goldfish.

"I've got him!" he yelled triumphantly.

"No, you haven't!" the
other goblins taunted,
as Flash wriggled free
from the goblin's grasp
and swam on.

"He's too slippery,"
the golfer goblin
grumbled.

"No, you're
too stupid!" the
fishing-net goblin
retorted rudely.
"Watch me catch
him." He jumped into
the air and grabbed
Flash. But once again
the goldfish slipped
easily through his fingers.

"You two are idiots!" roared one
of the other goblins. "Out of
my way!" He elbowed them
aside and leapt at Flash.
For a moment he held
the fish in his hands,
but then Flash
slithered free once
more. The goblin
made another grab,
but this time he
only managed to hit
himself on the nose.
"Ow!" he moaned.
Rachel and Kirsty
grinned at Molly, who
winked at them. "This
way, Flash!" she called,
holding out the sparkling fishbowl.

Flash headed straight towards the
bowl. As he swam, he magically
changed in size and shape until he was
fairy pet-sized again. Then he swam
neatly into his bowl.

"Good boy!" Molly said happily.

Rachel nudged Kirsty. "What are the goblins up to now?" she whispered anxiously.

"I don't know," Kirsty replied, frowning.

The goblins were huddled together, whispering to each other. Then, all of a sudden, they rushed towards the pond. Puzzled, Molly and the girls watched as the golfer goblin grabbed the fishing-net. He bent over the pond, dipping the net in the water, while the others crowded round him.

One of the other goblins took off his hat and began dipping that in the pond too.

"What are they doing?" Kirsty asked, as the goblins splashed about at the edge of the pond. But the next moment the goblin lifted his hat up out of the water and emptied it into the jam jar.

"Oh, no!" Kirsty gasped, as she saw a white fish with red spots tumble out of the hat and into the jar. "They've got Clown!"

"Look, we've got this teeny-tiny fish," one of the goblins in a kilt shouted, waving the jar at Molly and the girls. "And we're not giving it back unless you hand over Flash!"

Kirsty's Challenge

The girls and Molly stared at each other in dismay.

"They want us to swap Flash for Clown!" Rachel whispered.

Flash was swimming round in circles in his fishbowl, looking very anxious. He rose to the surface of the water, opened his mouth and a stream of

magical, multi-coloured bubbles poured
out. Molly listened closely.

"Flash wants us to hand him over,"
she said, biting her lip. "He says it's his
job to make sure poor Clown is safe."

"There must be another way to get
Clown back," Rachel said anxiously.

Meanwhile, Kirsty was thinking hard.
She knew it didn't take much to start
the goblins arguing amongst themselves.
All of a sudden, an idea popped into
her head.

"There is!" Kirsty whispered, excitedly. She marched over to the pond. The goblins glared at her and immediately formed a protective circle around the goblin with the jam jar.

"Look, we're all stuck," Kirsty said boldly. "You won't give up Clown..."

"No, we won't!" the goblins agreed.

"And we're not giving up Flash!" Kirsty went on firmly.

The goblins frowned.

"So let's have a competition," Kirsty said. "How about a tug-of-war? You goblins against us girls and Molly. The winning team gets both fish!"

The goblins stared uncertainly at Kirsty. Then, as she walked back to Rachel, Molly and Flash, they began whispering again.

"A tug-of-war?" Rachel asked, looking at Kirsty in confusion. "Do you really think we can win, Kirsty?"

Kirsty nodded. "The goblins will start arguing, just like they always do," she whispered. "They won't work together as a team; so they won't win!"

Molly brightened
immediately.
"I like it!" she
said, beaming.
Flash popped up
out of his fishbowl
and sent a stream
of colourful bubbles
towards Kirsty.

"Flash likes it too!" Molly told her.

The golfer goblin stepped forwards
and scowled at Kirsty. "A tug-of-war
isn't fair," he snapped. "We're all
different sizes."

"No problem," Molly said breezily.
"I can use my magic to make us all the
same size – if you goblins will agree to
keep still so that I can wave my wand
over you, that is."

Kirsty glanced at Rachel. They knew that the fairies could only cast spells on the goblins if they were standing still.

The goblins looked interested. They started whispering again, but this time they were so excited that Rachel, Kirsty and Molly could hear what they were saying.

"It'll be five of us against three of them," the golfer goblin said confidently. "We can't lose!"

"He's right," chuckled one of the kilt-wearing goblins. "We're much stronger than a fairy and two silly girls! Let's do it!"

Tug-of-War

"We accept the challenge," the golfer goblin said, glaring at Molly and the girls. "But no tricks, mind! You must shrink us all at exactly the same time."

"No tricks," Molly agreed. "Put the jam jar down on the rock."

The goblins still looked suspicious, but they did as Molly said. Molly put

Flash's bowl down on
the grass, and Flash
immediately
jumped out and
swam over to keep
Clown company.

"Ready?" Molly
called, lifting her wand.

Kirsty took a quick look down the
garden to make sure no one was
watching, and she was relieved to see
that they were well out of sight of her
parents and the Wainwrights. "Ready!"
she agreed, and Rachel nodded.

"Get on with it!" the golfer goblin
said rudely.

Molly waved her wand and a light
shower of turquoise fairy dust swirled
and sparkled around Rachel, Kirsty and

the goblins. The two girls caught
their breath as they immediately
shrank down to fairy-size. So did the
goblins, who looked down at themselves
in disgust.

"I hate being fairy-sized!" the
fishing-net goblin grumbled.

"It'll be worth it when we win," the
golfer goblin said boastfully.

Meanwhile, Molly had waved her wand again. This time a long, shiny blue rope appeared on the grass. Then a sparkly line of golden glitter appeared across the middle of the rope, to divide it into two equal sections.

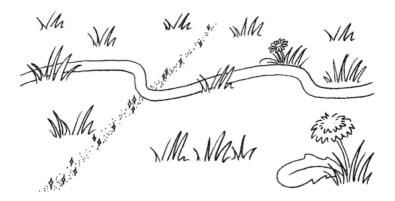

"The winning team is the one that manages to pull the other over the line," Molly announced, fluttering over to join the girls. "Shall we begin?"

"No!" snapped the golfer goblin. "We have to discuss our team tactics." He picked up one end of the rope. "I'm going at the front."

The goblin who'd caught Flash tried to grab the rope from him. "No, I want to be at the front!" he roared.

"You should be at the back," one of the kilt-wearing goblins chimed in, "You're the biggest."

"He's the biggest idiot, you mean!" said the golfer goblin scornfully. "Now, let's get on with it."

59

Kirsty glanced sideways at Rachel, trying not to smile; the goblins were arguing already, and they hadn't even started yet! "Let's go over the rules once more," Molly said. "Whoever wins the tug-of-war gets both fish."

The goblins nodded impatiently. Kirsty picked up the other end of the rope, with Rachel behind her. Then Molly waved her wand, and three fairy sparklers appeared next to the pond.

"Those sparklers are our starting system," Molly explained. "When the third one shoots glitter into the air, we start tugging!" She put down her wand and took hold of the rope behind Rachel.

"Get ready," yelled the golfer goblin, who was at the front of his team.

Whoosh! The first sparkler burst into life, sending red sparkles everywhere. A second later the next one sent out a swirl of amber glitter.

"Get ready!" Kirsty whispered to Rachel and Molly. Whoosh! The third sparkler sent green glitter flying into the air.

Immediately the girls and Molly began to pull with all their might. So did the goblins. At first the contest was very even. Neither team could get the other towards the line. But the goblins did have two pairs of extra arms. At last, very slowly, they began to pull Molly and the girls towards the line, a little bit at a time.

Flash was looking very anxious as he swam round and round in the air, and Kirsty's heart sank. She dug her heels into the lawn, trying to hold on, but it was very difficult. She could hear Molly and Rachel panting behind her.

"We're winning!" yelled the golfer goblin gleefully. "Come on, pull harder!"

He gave the rope a huge tug. As he did so, he stepped back onto the toe of the goblin behind him.

"Ow!" shrieked the goblin, letting go of the rope. "You clumsy fool!" And he poked the golfer goblin sharply in the back.

The golfer goblin spun round, letting go of the rope too. "Who are you calling a fool?" he snarled.

"Don't let go!" shouted the other three goblins furiously.

"Don't tell me what to do!" yelled the golfer goblin sulkily, shoving the one behind him.

"Pull as hard as you can!" Kirsty whispered to Rachel and Molly, as all five goblins started squabbling.

The girls and Molly began to heave at the rope. To their delight, they saw that they were dragging the arguing goblins closer and closer to the sparkling golden line.

Winner Takes All

At first the goblins didn't notice.

Then suddenly the golfer goblin gave a cry of rage. "We're losing! Pull harder!"

The goblins stopped fighting, but two of them had lost their grip on the rope. As they struggled to get hold of it again, the girls and Molly pulled them even closer to the line.

"You're not trying!" yelled the golfer
goblin, who was red in the face.
He strained at the rope, and
managed to pull Kirsty
a little way towards him.
But in doing so, he
poked the goblin
behind him hard
in the ribs with
his elbow.

"Aargh!" The goblin
dropped the rope and
doubled over in pain.

"Idiot!" shouted the
one behind him crossly,
taking one hand off the
rope to give him a shove.

"We've got them now!"
Kirsty panted. "PULL!"

The golfer goblin's big green toes were almost on the line. With one mighty effort, the girls and Molly yanked him across to their side. Although they tried to dig their heels in, the other goblins came tumbling after him, one by one. "We won!" Kirsty cried. The goblins were looking very shocked and very grumpy. Straight away they started arguing about which one of them was to blame. "The contest is over!" Molly announced firmly, picking up her wand. "Give Clown back, please."

"No!" snapped the golfer goblin.

Kirsty and Rachel looked at each other in dismay.

"The contest wasn't fair!" the golfer goblin continued.

"Of course it was fair!" Rachel gasped.

"And you agreed to the rules!" Kirsty pointed out.

"We don't care. We're not giving the fish back!" the golfer goblin told them, and the other goblins cheered.

"Well!" Molly put her hands on her hips. "I knew goblins were mean and naughty, but this is just too bad!" Then she smiled at Rachel and Kirsty. "Don't worry, girls," she went on, "I have an idea."

And with a flick of her
wand, she sent a swirl
of magic fairy dust
towards Rachel and
Kirsty. In the blink
of an eye, the two
girls were back to
their normal size.

"Go and get Clown, girls," Molly
said, her green eyes dancing merrily.
"After all, we won the contest fair
and square!"

"Hey!" shouted the golfer goblin,
jumping up and down angrily. His
voice was so tiny, Rachel and Kirsty
could hardly hear what he was saying.

"You can't do that! Stop them!"
The tiny, fairy-sized goblins scurried
over as Rachel and Kirsty headed for

the jam jar. But they were too small to stop the girls. Kirsty carefully tipped Clown back into the pond, and he swam away happily. Flash watched, looking very pleased, and then swam back to his fishbowl, shimmering and shining happily. Molly picked up the bowl, blew a kiss to Flash and then flew down to the goblins.

"You should have kept to our agreement!" she said, shaking her head. She waved her wand again. Rachel and Kirsty watched as the goblin's fishing-net lifted magically from the rock and drifted towards the goblins, surrounded by sparkling magic.

It floated down over them, trapping all the goblins underneath.

"Help!" they shouted furiously. "Let us out!"

"You'll find a way to escape when you learn to work together," Molly told them.

"What will happen to them?" asked Rachel quietly.

Molly grinned. "My spell will wear off in a little while and then the goblins will be their normal size again," she replied. "But by then I will have taken Flash back to Fairyland, so the other fish will be quite safe. And the goblins will have to hurry back to Jack Frost and tell him they've failed once more."

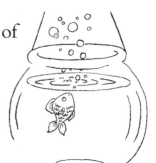

Flash swam to the top of his fishbowl and shiny rainbow-coloured bubbles poured from his open mouth.

"Flash says thank you for all your help, girls," Molly translated, "and so do I." She glanced at the goblins, who were still arguing under the fishing-net. "They won't cause any more trouble, so go and enjoy your barbecue," she said, waving at the girls.

"Goodbye!" she cried, blowing the girls a kiss as she vanished in a swirl of sparkles.

Kirsty beamed at Rachel. "Wasn't Flash gorgeous?" she said. "I'm so glad Molly's got him back."

"Me too," Rachel agreed. "Now we've

only got one magic pet left to find. And only one more day before I have to go home!"

Kirsty nodded. "I do hope we find Penny the Pony Fairy's magic pet tomorrow," she said.

"Girls!" Mrs Tate called suddenly from the patio. "The food's ready."

"Great!" said Kirsty eagerly. "I'm starving after that tug-of-war!"

"So am I," Rachel laughed. "We really worked up an appetite!" And she and Kirsty hurried off up the garden, leaving the grumbling goblins behind.

Win a Rainbow Magic
Sparkly T-Shirt and Goody Bag!

In every book in the Rainbow Magic Pet Keeper Fairies series (books 29-35) there is a hidden picture of a collar with a secret letter in it. Find all seven letters and re-arrange them to make a special Fairyland word, then send it to us. Each month we will put the entries into a draw and select one winner to receive a Rainbow Magic Sparkly T-shirt and Goody Bag!

Send your entry on a postcard to Rainbow Magic Pet Keeper Competition, Orchard Books, 338 Euston Road, London NW1 3BH. Australian readers should write to Hachette Children's Books, Level 17/207 Kent Street, Sydney, NSW 2000.
Don't forget to include your name and address.
Only one entry per child. Final draw: 30th April 2007.

Good luck!

Don't miss...
Kylie the Carnival Fairy

1-84616-175-4

Kylie the Carnival Fairy needs Kirsty's and Rachel's help! Jack Frost has stolen the three magic hats that make the Sunnydays Carnival so much fun, and the girls have to get them back...

Have you checked out the

website at:

www.rainbowmagic.co.uk

There are games, activities and fun things to do, as well as news and information about Rainbow Magic and all of the fairies.

by Daisy Meadows

The Rainbow Fairies

Ruby the Red Fairy	ISBN	1 84362 016 2
Amber the Orange Fairy	ISBN	1 84362 017 0
Saffron the Yellow Fairy	ISBN	1 84362 018 9
Fern the Green Fairy	ISBN	1 84362 019 7
Sky the Blue Fairy	ISBN	1 84362 020 0
Izzy the Indigo Fairy	ISBN	1 84362 021 9
Heather the Violet Fairy	ISBN	1 84362 022 7

The Weather Fairies

Crystal the Snow Fairy	ISBN	1 84362 633 0
Abigail the Breeze Fairy	ISBN	1 84362 634 9
Pearl the Cloud Fairy	ISBN	1 84362 635 7
Goldie the Sunshine Fairy	ISBN	1 84362 641 1
Evie the Mist Fairy	ISBN	1 84362 636 5
Storm the Lightning Fairy	ISBN	1 84362 637 3
Hayley the Rain Fairy	ISBN	1 84362 638 1

The Party Fairies

Cherry the Cake Fairy	ISBN	1 84362 818 X
Melodie the Music Fairy	ISBN	1 84362 819 8
Grace the Glitter Fairy	ISBN	1 84362 820 1
Honey the Sweet Fairy	ISBN	1 84362 821 X
Polly the Party Fun Fairy	ISBN	1 84362 822 8
Phoebe the Fashion Fairy	ISBN	1 84362 823 6
Jasmine the Present Fairy	ISBN	1 84362 824 4

The Jewel Fairies

India the Moonstone Fairy	ISBN	1 84362 958 5
Scarlett the Garnet Fairy	ISBN	1 84362 954 2
Emily the Emerald Fairy	ISBN	1 84362 955 0
Chloe the Topaz Fairy	ISBN	1 84362 956 9
Amy the Amethyst Fairy	ISBN	1 84362 957 7
Sophie the Sapphire Fairy	ISBN	1 84362 953 4
Lucy the Diamond Fairy	ISBN	1 84362 959 3

The Pet Keeper Fairies

Katie the Kitten Fairy	ISBN	1 84616 166 5
Bella the Bunny Fairy	ISBN	1 84616 170 3
Georgia the Guinea Pig Fairy	ISBN	1 84616 168 1
Lauren the Puppy Fairy	ISBN	1 84616 169 X
Harriet the Hamster Fairy	ISBN	1 84616 167 3
Molly the Goldfish Fairy	ISBN	1 84616 172 X
Penny the Pony Fairy	ISBN	1 84616 171 1
Holly the Christmas Fairy	ISBN	1 84362 661 6
Summer the Holiday Fairy	ISBN	1 84362 960 7
Stella the Star Fairy	ISBN	1 84362 869 4
Kylie the Carnival Fairy	ISBN	1 84616 175 4
The Rainbow Magic Treasury	ISBN	1 84616 047 2

All priced at £3.99. *Holly the Christmas Fairy, Summer the Holiday Fairy,
Stella the Star Fairy* and *Kylie the Carnival Fairy* are priced at £4.99.
The Rainbow Magic Treasury is priced at £12.99.
Rainbow Magic books are available from all good bookshops, or can be ordered
direct from the publisher: Orchard Books, PO BOX 29, Douglas IM99 1BQ
Credit card orders please telephone 01624 836000
or fax 01624 837033 or visit our Internet site: www.wattspub.co.uk
or e-mail: bookshop@enterprise.net for details.

To order please quote title, author and ISBN and your full name and address.
Cheques and postal orders should be made payable to 'Bookpost plc.'
Postage and packing is FREE within the UK
(overseas customers should add £2.00 per book).
Prices and availability are subject to change.

Look out for the Fun Day Fairies!

MEGAN THE MONDAY FAIRY
1-84616-188-6

TALLULAH THE TUESDAY FAIRY
1-84616-189-4

WILLOW THE WEDNESDAY FAIRY
1-84616-190-8

THEA THE THURSDAY FAIRY
1-84616-191-6

FREYA THE FRIDAY FAIRY
1-84616-192-4

SIENNA THE SATURDAY FAIRY
1-84616-193-2

SARAH THE SUNDAY FAIRY
1-84616-194-0

Available from
Saturday 2nd September 2006